To the memory of my father, Winfield D. Bootman.
For the spirit of steel pan music; the staff at PS 274 in
Bushwick, Brooklyn; George & Sushi; and, finally,
for Keith A. Jones, without whose ceaseless help this
book would not have been possible
—C.B.

Text copyright © 2009 by Colin Bootman
Illustrations copyright © 2009 by Colin Bootman

Carolrhoda Books
A division of Lerner Publishing Group, Inc.
241 First Avenue North
Minneapolis, MN 55401 USA

Website address: www.lernerbooks.com

Library of Congress Cataloging-in-Publication Data

Bootman, Colin.
  The steel pan man of Harlem / written and illustrated by Colin Bootman.
    p.   cm.
  Summary: A mysterious man appears in Harlem and promises to rid the city of its
rats by playing the steel pan drum.
  ISBN: 978–0–8225–9026–2 (lib. bdg. : alk. paper)
  [1. Rats—Fiction. 2. Steel drum (Musical instrument)—Fiction. 3. Harlem (New
York, N.Y.)—Fiction.] I. Title.
PZ7.B32446St 2009
[E]—dc22   2008039654

Manufactured in the United States of America
1 2 3 4 5 6 – DP – 14 13 12 11 10 09

The
Steel
Pan
Man
of
Harlem

Colin Bootman

 Carolrhoda Books Minneapolis · New York

ONCE UPON A TIME IN THE CITY OF HARLEM, there was a terrible problem. Rats were everywhere!

They crowded the subways, the restaurants, the office buildings, the stores and, worst of all, the homes of all Harlem citizens. They slept in beds, ate at dinner tables, and relaxed in living rooms. They even swam in bathtubs.

The citizens of Harlem were fed up. Something had to be done! Traps were set, but the rats were too clever. The people of Harlem chased the rats and called the exterminator, but the rats were too fast and too many.

Finally, the citizens, the council, and the exterminator all went to the mayor. They asked very sternly, "What are you going to do about these rats?" The mayor didn't know. But he knew the citizens were angry and frustrated.

WEEKS LATER, a stranger appeared at the busy 125½ Street subway station. People stared as the stranger stood in the middle of the platform holding a strange round red case.

The stranger opened his case and took out
a shiny, round steel pan. Everyone watched as
he mounted the steel pan on stands and then
pulled two wooden sticks from his back pocket.
He held the sticks in the air, closed his eyes,
and began playing the sweetest melody anyone
had ever heard.

His hands moved like magic. All around the stranger, fingers snapped, feet tapped, and hands clapped. The dancing people bobbed and swung and weaved. Even the rats were charmed by the sweet melody. Suddenly the music stopped. Snapped out of its trance, the crowd watched the stranger pack up his case and leave the station.

The stranger walked straight to the mayor's office. After many hours, the mayor finally called him in. The stranger bowed and introduced himself. "Good day, Mayor," he said cheerfully. "I am called the Steel Pan Man."

The mayor and his kitty looked the stranger up and down. "I can play many melodies," said the pan man. "Some are for dancing. Some are for marching. Some will make you happy. Some will make you sad. I can play a melody that will solve your rat problem."

The mayor was desperate. And he wanted to keep
his job, so he listened. The pan man continued,
"I will rid your city of all the rats for a fee of one
million dollars."

"A million dollars!" gasped the mayor. "That's
way too much money!"

The pan man was nearly out the door when the mayor called him back. He had no choice. "If you can rid the city of these disgusting rats, I will pay your fee."

"Well then," said the pan man, "I will need an empty barge. And you will have to shut down all the subways, roads, tunnels, and bridges by this evening."

"Agreed," said the mayor, and they shook hands.

LATER THAT NIGHT, the Steel Pan Man stood in the middle of the garbage barge. He held his two sticks in the air, tapped them together three times, closed his eyes and began playing another sweet melody.

He played his strange shiny instrument, his hands moving like magic.

Pa da ding Pa da ding Pa da ding ding

Soon the rats started climbing out of the sewers.
By the tens of thousands. Dancing to the music.
All the rats could be seen. They came from all
directions in all colors and sizes. The rats
pushed and tripped over one another as
the music played. Soon the docks
were filled with rats.

Pa da ding

ding dong

Pa da ding

Pa da ding

ding dong

ding

dong

Pa da ding

ding

dong

They squealed and scratched as they climbed aboard the garbage barge. By the time they realized what had happened, the barge had already set sail while the pan man stood safely on the docks.

THE NEXT MORNING, everyone in Harlem rejoiced. Not a single rat was seen. The pan man returned to the mayor's office.

"Good day, Mayor," said the pan man cheerfully. "I have come to collect my money."

"What money?" replied the mayor. "Do you know how much it cost to shut down the city so you could play a few notes on that thing of yours?" asked the mayor very angrily.

The pan man's eyes were no longer cheerful.
He turned and walked away.

Pa ba ba ding Pa ding pa ding ding

The pan man walked to the middle of 125½ Street, mounted his steel pan on its stands, and began playing the sweetest melody yet.

ing ding dong ba ding ding ding dong ding

The citizens of Harlem came from every direction.
They poured out of office buildings, subways,
restaurants, and homes. Children tumbled out
of schools, parks, and playgrounds. Soon the
streets of Harlem were filled with people.

A magical spell had been cast, and the people could not stop themselves from dancing. They twirled and jumped and twisted with glee. The people of Harlem danced until they were tired and breathless. But the pan man played on, and the people kept dancing.

ding Pa da ding Pa da ding ding ding dong

No one was spared the pan man's magic, including the mayor.
He danced out of his office, his kitty right beside him. Like a
puppet, the mayor made his way through the crowded streets.
Jerking and twisting, he finally reached the pan man. "Stop.
Please. Stop," he rasped, waving a check for one million dollars.
"Can't keep dancing. I'll pay you. As agreed."

Everyone now knew that the mayor was responsible for the spell cast on the city. Then suddenly, the music stopped. The pan man wiped his brow and put his sticks into his back pocket.

The spell was broken. But the mayor's feet were
still moving. It was as if his legs had minds of
their own. They did the the fox-trot, the bolero,
the Charleston. . . . He danced all the way down
125½ Street and out of Harlem. The mayor was
never seen again.

THE STEEL PAN MAN packed his pan, and he, too, left Harlem.

Author's Note

When I was seven, I moved from Trinidad to the United States and started school in the second grade. On Tuesdays, my teacher, Ms. Bloom, took the class to the library for "read aloud." For me, this was the best time of the week. I loved storytelling. Once Ms. White, the librarian, read *The Pied Piper of Hamelin* by Robert Browning to my class. While Ms. White was reading, her assistant played the flute. I was hooked from the first note. Browning's poem impressed me so much that when I decided to do a picture book about the steel drum, I knew it had to be done through a retelling of this classic story.

The steel drum, or steel pan, is widely accepted to have been invented in the Caribbean during the Carnival seasons of the late 1930s. I grew up listening to steel pan music, courtesy of my uncles, Wilfred and Randolph St. Louis, who led steel orchestras in Trinidad in the 1970s and 1980s. The pan eventually became Trinidad's national instrument and a symbol of Caribbean unity and culture.

I chose Harlem for the setting of my story because—aside from the fact that the name sounds close to Hamelin—most Caribbean folks immigrated to Harlem during the 1920s, 1930s, and 1940s. This period was a musical time. As far as music and dance go, Harlem had a little something for everyone. Swing, the jitterbug, and the samba filled the dance halls. And Caribbean immigrants introduced the celebration of Carnival.

The Steel Pan Man of Harlem tries to capture the spirit of Carnival, dance, and music through its lively dance scenes. And though my version is not as dark as Browning's poem, I would like to think I held fast to his original message: the importance of doing the right thing and keeping one's word.